First published in the United States of America in 2014 by Chronicle Books LLC. Originally published in Germany in 2011 and 2012 by Verlagshaus Jacoby & Stuart GmbH under the titles *Das 24-Stunden-Wimmelbuch: In der Stadt ist was los!*, *Das 24-Stunden-Wimmelbuch: Auf dem Bauernhof ist was los!*, and *Das 24-Stunden-Wimmelbuch: Am Hafen ist was los!*.

Library of Congress Cataloging-in-Publication Data available.
ISBN 978-1-4521-1700-3

Manufactured in China.

Design by Amy Yu Gray.
Typeset in Chic Hand and Omnes.

10 9 8 7 6 5 4 3 2 1

Chronicle Books LLC
680 Second Street, San Francisco, California 94107

Chronicle Books—we see things differently. Become part
of our community at www.chroniclekids.com.

Britta Teckentrup

Busy Bunny Days

In the Town,
On the Farm
& At the Port

chronicle books · san francisco

Gary Gator

Gilly Gator

Kitty

Kiki Kiwi

Ellie

Gabby Gator   Harold Hippo

Dr. Bunny

Mrs. Bunny

Baxter Bunny

Bethany Bunny

Grandma Bunny

Vincent

Dotty and Daniel

Baker Bear

Evan

Mr. Wuff

Baby Wuff

Ruby Rhino

Charlie the Chimney Sweep

Benny Badger

Bernhard Builder

Spot

Barbara Bear

Margo Mare

Sputnik   Oskar

Heidi Hound

Mrs. Katz

Lilly Katz

Howard Hound

Linus

Laura

Veronica Vogue

Los Andinos

In the town…

Join the Bunny family for a busy day in their hometown, surrounded by friends and neighbors! From the time they wake up until the time they go to sleep, there is so much to see and do. But don't forget to keep an eye out for that pesky Benny Badger—he is always up to no good!

Rise and shine! It is 6 o'clock in the morning, and it's time to wake up!

- How are Bethany, Baxter, Mrs., and Dr. Bunny getting ready for their day?
- Oh no! Who is slipping on a banana peel?
- Where is that lazy Benny Badger?

Hurry, hurry! It is 9 o'clock in the morning, and school is starting!

• What happens at home while Bethany and Baxter are on their way to school?
• Who is walking Bethany to kindergarten?
• Who is Baxter's best friend?

CAFE

Grab an umbrella! It is 12 o'clock, and the rain is rolling into town!

- What is that sneaky Benny Badger doing while Baker Bear's back is turned?
- What kind of doctor is Dr. Bunny? Who is his patient?
- Who is Baxter's teacher?

DYNAMO
ICYCLE FACTORY

ELEMENTARY SCHOOL

boutique

KIOSK

KERY

kindergarten

Yum, yum! It is 3 o'clock in the afternoon, and it's time for a snack.

• What is Mrs. Bunny doing?
• How is Barbara Bear doing after her fall earlier this morning?
• Uh-oh! What has Heidi Hound left on the balcony?

CAFÉ

Quick! Call the fire department! It is 5 o'clock in the evening, and there is quite a commotion!

- Whose home has caught fire? How did the fire start?
- What is that pesky Benny Badger up to while everyone is distracted?
- Who has come to visit the Bunny family?

Scrub-a-dub-dub! It is 7 o'clock in the evening, and the Bunny family is settling in for the night.

- What is happening at the school, now that all the students have gone home?
- Oh dear! What caused the leak in the Bunny residence?
- What are Baxter and Bethany doing before bed?

CAFE

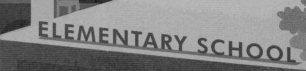

What an eventful day! It is 9 o'clock at night, and almost everyone is asleep . . .

• That Benny Badger has been up to no good all day! Who finally helped catch him?
• Why is Baxter sleeping in the living room?
• What are Dr. and Mrs. Bunny doing?

DYNAMO
BICYCLE FACTORY

ELEMENTARY SCHOOL

BAKERY

KIOSK

kindergarten

POLICE

Nigel

Logan

Tabby

Sputnik

Oskar

Gloria Gardiner

Graham Gardiner

Benny Badger

Mrs. Bunny

Dr. Bunny

Grandma Bunny

Baxter Bunny

Bethany Bunny

Ellie

Gracie Gardiner

Garrett Gardiner

Grandpa Bear

Benji Bear

Bella Bear

Mama Bear

Papa Bear

Ranger Roger

Scout

Willy Wolf

Mrs. Brown

Carter

Postman Pete

Ana

Ariana

On the farm...

The Bunny family and Bethany's best friend, Ellie, are visiting their friends, the Gardiners, on a fun-filled farm adventure! See what happens from dawn to dusk out in the country. But don't lose track of that unruly Benny Badger as he sneaks around the farm!

Cock-a-doodle-do! It is 6 o'clock in the morning, and the farm is already buzzing with activity!

• Who is already awake and working hard?
• What is **Mama Bear** tinkering with by the garden?
• Find that lazy **Benny Badger**!

Up and at 'em! It is 9 o'clock in the morning, and it's time to get to work!

- What is **Mama Bear** doing?
- Where did **Dr.** and **Mrs. Bunny** go this morning?
- Why is **Grandpa Bear** resting?

Grab some gardening gloves! It is 12 o'clock, and it's time to tend to the vegetable patch!

- Who is keeping **Grandma Bunny** company?
- Who has a letter for **Postman Pete**?
- Where are **Bethany** and **Ellie** playing hide-and-seek?

What a nice day! It is 3 o'clock in the afternoon, and it's time for some fun in the sun.

- Where are the two places to swim on the farm? Who is swimming where?
- What are the other kids doing for fun?
- Find that sneaky **Benny Badger**!

Come and get it! It is 5 o'clock in the evening, and it's time to eat!

- Who is setting the table for dinner?
- Uh-oh! Who is getting a snack who shouldn't be?
- Where are all the cows going?

It's a party! It is 7 o'clock in the evening, and it's time to dance!

- What did Ranger Roger give to Baxter?
- What has Willy Wolf discovered in the hayloft?
- Where is that pesky Benny Badger?

What a busy day on the farm! It is 9 o'clock at night, and *almost* everyone is asleep . . .

- What was that no-good Benny Badger caught stealing?
- Which baby animal was just born?
- Who is still playing in the tent?

Orlando Otter

Oliver Otter

Peter Puffin

Benny Badger

Bailey Bear

Scout

Grandpa Bear

Christian

Caleb

Craig

Mrs. Bunny

Dr. Bunny

Pippa

Lia

Mr. Mallard

Baxter Bunny

Grandma Bunny

Bethany Bunny

Ellie

Mrs. Mallard

Vincent

Fiona Fisher

Franklin Fisher

Sally Bird

Toby Turtle

Sailor Seth

Squawk

Tomcat

Cindy Bird

Sailor Sal

Captain Nemo

Sammy Seal

Timothy Tiger

Patricia Penguin

Edgar Eagle

Crane Operator Ken

Edwin Eagle

Henry Hound

William Walrus

Pam Puffin

Little Eddie Eagle

Alyson Albatross

At the port...

Follow along with the Bunny family and their friends as they enjoy an exciting day at the port! From early morning until late at night, the docks are bustling with all kinds of activity. But be sure not to lose track of that no-good Benny Badger in all the hustle and hubbub down on the docks!

Ahoy, mateys! It is 6 o'clock in the morning, and the port is already bustling with activity!

- What is **Bailey Bear** going to do down at the docks?
- Did **Henry Hound** catch anything worthwhile?
- Find that sneaky **Benny Badger**!

Land ho! It is 9 o'clock in the morning, and a new ship has pulled into port!

• Who has joined the Bunny family on their trip to the port?
• What are Fiona and Franklin Fisher unloading from their boat?
• Has Squawk made a friend?

Got a grumbling tummy? It is 12 o'clock, and it's time for lunch!

- What are the tickets from the ticket booth good for?
- What is spilling out of the yellow shipping crate?
- What is Mrs. Mallard doing?

Grab an umbrella! It is 3 o'clock in the afternoon, and it has started to rain!

- What kind of boat is helping Peter Puffin?
- How many umbrellas are there?
- Where did Benny Badger take cover during the storm?

POSEIDON
PANAMA

TICKETS

How beautiful! It is 5 o'clock in the evening, and the sun is setting over the water.

• Baxter and Scout are standing really still. What could they be doing?
• What's happening on the pirate ship?
• Where is Henry Hound fishing now?

TICKETS

All aboard! It is 7 o'clock in the evening, and it's time to set sail!

- What are Mr. and Mrs. Mallard doing?
- Where is that no-good Benny Badger hiding?
- Who is getting their picture taken before they board the cruise ship?

TICKETS

Bon voyage! It is 9 o'clock at night, and the cruise ship is leaving the port!

• Did that pesky **Benny Badger** get away with his stowaway scheme?
• Who is in the ticket booth now?
• What is **Bailey Bear** doing?